CHICKABELLA
SHAPES UP

Words by
Veronica Strachan

Pictures by
Cassi Strachan

First published 2021 by Veronica & Cassi Strachan. We acknowledge the Wurundjeri people who are the Traditional Custodians of the Land on which we live, and pay our respects to Elders past, present and emerging who have been telling their stories for tens of thousands of years.

Paperback ISBN-13: 978-0-6488377-4-9

Ebook ISBN-13: 978-0-6488377-5-6

A catalogue record for this book is available from the National Library of Australia

For children of all shapes and sizes

Chickabella was always the last one into bed.

Her seven younger siblings raced her to the chook shed and got the best spots to snuggle up in.

Chickabella wanted to snuggle with her mum. But her younger siblings were all in better shape.

"How do you shape up? Chickabella asked her siblings.

"I like running in a circle," said Ren.

"I like flapping in a triangle," said Oliver.

"I like walking in a star," said Youssef.

"I like jumping in a diamond," said Gaurav.

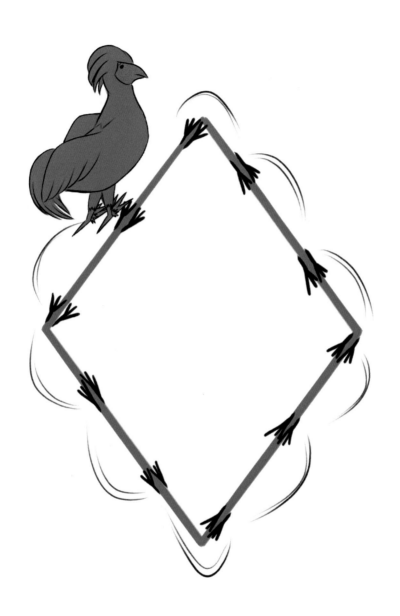

"I like squatting in a square," said Bennett.

"I like skipping in a rectangle," said Inala.

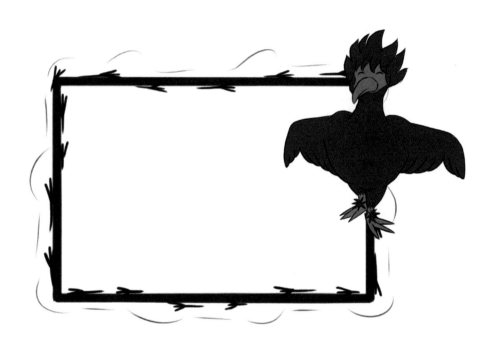

"I like hopping in an oval," said Vena.

"How do you shape up, Mum?" asked Chickabella.

"I like hugging in a heart," said Chickabella's Mum.

"Me too," said Chickabella.

What's **your** favourite way to shape up?

Can you see any shapes around you, right now?

Be on the lookout for more of Chickabella's adventures.

Other titles in the "The Adventures of Chickabella" series:

Chickabella and the Rainbow Magic

Chickabella Counts to Ten

If you enjoyed reading Chickabella Shapes Up, please tell your friends all about it, and consider leaving us a review on Amazon, Goodreads or your favourite online bookstore.

Your few words can make a real difference.

You can read more about Chickabella and other books by Veronica Strachan at
www.veronicastrachan.com.au

You can see more drawings by Cassi Strachan at
www.creativegirltuesday.com.au

Made in the USA
Las Vegas, NV
09 November 2022

59026627R00021